JUDITH CASELEY

Greenwillow Books New York

Library of Congress Cataloging-in-Publication Data

Caseley, Judith.
The noisemakers / by Judith Caseley.
p.   cm.
Summary: The mothers of two rambunctious, noisy
children find the perfect place for them to play.
ISBN 0-688-09394-9. ISBN 0-688-09395-7 (lib. bdg.)
[1. Play—Fiction.   2. Noise—Fiction.]   I. Title.
PZ7.C2677No   1992   [E]—dc20
90-2806   CIP   AC

To baby Michael,
my newest noisemaker

_S_am and Laura liked noise.
Lots of noise.

Sam made believe he was an airplane.
He roared, very loudly.
"Can't you be a quiet plane?" asked his mother.
"No," said Sam. And he roared some more.

Laura made believe she was a monster.
She flapped her arms and shouted, "Grrrr!" very loudly.
"Can't you be a quiet monster?" asked her mother.
"No," said Laura. And she growled some more.

At Sam's house, Laura pretended
she was a jack-in-the-box.
"Pop!" shouted Laura.
"Pop!" shouted Sam.
"POP POP POP POP!" they shouted together.
"Can't you be quiet jack-in-the-boxes?"
said Laura's mother.
"No!" said Laura and Sam.

At Laura's house, Sam pretended he was a cow.
"Moo, moo, mooooo!" he said loudly.
Laura was a rooster.
"Cock-a-doodle-dooooo!" she crowed.
"How about being quiet animals?"
said Sam's mother.
"Meow," said Sam.
"Peep peep!" said Laura.

One day Sam and Laura and
their mothers went to the library.
Laura read a book about a giant.
"Fee, fi, fo, fum," she shouted.
"Ho, ho, ho," answered Sam.
"Shhhhh," said Laura's mother.

Sam read a book about a drum.
"Rat-a-tat-tat," said Sam.
"Boom boom boom," said Laura.
"Shhh," said Sam's mother.
"Rat-a-tat-tat and boom boom boom!"
shouted Laura and Sam.

"We prefer quiet reading,"
said the librarian.
"See?" said Laura's mother.
"See?" said Sam's mother.
"Boom!" said Laura.
"Rat-a-tat-tat!" said Sam.
They left the library.

They went into a restaurant.
Sam and Laura had
grilled cheese sandwiches with pickles.
Their mothers had French toast.
Laura clinked her cup of milk
against Sam's.
"To Sam," she said.
"To Laura," he said, clinking back.

They clinked their spoons.
They clinked their pickles.
"To Laura," said Sam.
"To Sam," said Laura.
Then they clinked their
grilled cheese sandwiches.

"Stop," said Laura's mother.
"Enough," said Sam's mother.
"Grrrrr," growled Laura.
"Roarrrr," shouted Sam.
"My hearing aid!" said the lady
at the next table.

The manager put the bill on the table.
"You're disturbing my other customers,"
she said.
"See?" said Laura's mother.
"See?" said Sam's mother.
They left the restaurant.

They went into a department store.
Laura's mother tried on shoes.
Sam tried on shoes, too.
"Look at me!" said Sam.
"Look at me!" said Laura.
"Put the shoes back," said Sam's mother.
"We have to go," said Laura's mother.

Sam and Laura ran down the aisle.
"Slowly!" said Sam's mother.
"Use your walking shoes!" said Laura's mother.
"Gorillas don't wear walking shoes!"
 said Laura.
"Neither do airplanes!" said Sam.
"Ugh, ugh, ugh," said Laura.
"Zoom, zoom, zoom," said Sam.
"Out," said their mothers.

They found a bench and sat on it.
"I'm sorry," said Sam's mother,
"but airplanes don't belong in stores.
And monsters don't belong in restaurants."
"And giants don't belong in libraries!"
said Laura's mother.
"Where do they belong?" said Sam.
"Where do they belong?" said Laura.
Their mothers looked at each other.

"We'll show you," said Sam's mother.
"It's not far," said Laura's mother.
 They walked a little
 until they came to a gate.
 They went inside.

Sam was a gorilla
on top of the jungle gym.
Laura was a monster
on top of the slide.
They were monkeys on the swings
and chickens in the tunnel.
They screamed and growled
and shouted in the playground.

And their mothers thought
they were wonderful.